POPPY

the Pirate Dog

POPPY
the Pirate Dog

Liz Kessler

illustrated by Mike Phillips

CANDLEWICK PRESS

This book is dedicated
to the one and only real-life
Poppy the Pirate Dog.
L. K.

Text copyright © 2012 by Liz Kessler
Illustrations copyright © 2012 by Mike Phillips

First published in Great Britain by Orion Children's Books,
a division of the Orion Publishing Group

First U.S. paperback edition 2015

Library of Congress Catalog Card Number 2012947713
ISBN 978-0-7636-6569-2 (hardcover)
ISBN 978-0-7636-7661-2 (paperback)

16 17 18 19 APS 10 9 8 7 6 5 4 3 2

Printed in Humen, Dongguan, China

This book was typeset in Badger.
The illustrations were done in ink and watercolor.

Candlewick Press
99 Dover Street
Somerville, Massachusetts 02144

visit us at www.candlewick.com

Contents

Chapter One   1

Chapter Two   11

Chapter Three   19

Chapter Four   33

Chapter Five   45

CHAPTER
One

The Brown family was going on vacation. Mom, Dad, Tim, Suzy, and Poppy, their Dalmatian, were all going to the beach for a week.

When it was time to leave, Poppy
was out the door and galloping for
the car before you could say "Watch
the tulips!"

Dad laughed. "I guess we're ready to go," he said.

Poppy looked out the window as they drove, wagging her tail all the way.

As soon as they arrived, they decided to take a walk down to the harbor.

Poppy wagged her tail and picked up her leash, and off they went.

"Look — a hat shop!" Mom said as
they walked along the waterfront.

Tim and Suzy waited outside
with Poppy while Mom tried on lots
of hats.

Poppy had never been to the seaside before, so she wanted a closer look. She pulled and tugged on her leash, trying to see everything. Somehow she got it wrapped around one of the hat stands and almost knocked it over!

A scarf fell off the stand. It was black and white, with skulls and crossbones.

Poppy picked it up in her mouth. Then she looked at Suzy with her big brown eyes.

"You like this scarf, don't you?" Suzy asked.

Poppy wagged her tail.

So Dad bought the scarf for Poppy
and a new hat for Mom. Suzy tied the
scarf around Poppy's neck.

"Looks good," Mom said.
"Very nice," Dad agreed.

"She's a pirate!" Tim said.

"A pirate dog!" Suzy added.

"Poppy, the Pirate Dog!" they all said together.

CHAPTER
Two

Poppy knew all about pirates. Tim had five books about them, and she had spent many hours looking at the pictures with him.

Pirates were exciting, daring, and dangerous. And now she was, too!

She looked down her nose at other dogs who came to sniff and play with her as they walked along. *Don't mess with me,* she thought. *I'm a pirate dog.*

When they stopped at the end of
the pier to eat ice cream, she looked
out to sea. *I'm looking for my pirate
ship,* she thought. Pirate dogs *always*
have a pirate ship.

"Now what?" asked Dad as they finished their ice cream.

"Let's look at the notices on the wall and decide what to do this week," Mom said.

"Boat trips!" Suzy and Tim said as they read the notices.

"A fishing trip — that sounds good," Dad said.

"Seal spotting," said Mom. "That could be fun."

"Pedal boats!" shouted Suzy.

"Speedboat rides!" yelled Tim.

Mom and Dad looked at each other.

"Why don't we do them all?" Dad said. "One each day?"

Poppy wagged her tail so hard, she swatted a seagull.

Four boat trips! Life didn't get better than that for a pirate dog.

CHAPTER
Three

That night, Poppy dreamed about

adventures on the high seas.

With the wind in her ears and salt
on her lips, she stood at the bow of the

ship, looking ahead and pointing a
paw at the horizon.

The next morning, she was the first one up.

She sat by the door, wagging her tail.

Then she ran around in circles.

Then she went to Mom and Dad's
bed and let them know she was ready.

"Go away, Poppy. It's only six
o'clock!" Dad cried.

Finally, after breakfast, everybody went down to the harbor for the fishing trip.

When they reached the front of the line, the fishing-boat man took their tickets. "Will she be all right on the boat?" he asked, looking at Poppy.

"Well, she's never been on a boat before, but I'm sure she'll be fine," said Mom.

"Of course she'll be fine," Suzy said. "She's a pirate dog!"

Dad climbed onto the fishing boat. Mom went next. Tim followed, and Suzy came last with Poppy.

"Come on, Poppy," she said, gently tugging on Poppy's leash.

Poppy looked at the boat. It was bobbing up and down on the water. It sure moved a lot!

"I'll do it," Tim said. He took the leash and pulled.

Poppy sat down.

"Let me do it," Mom said. She took the leash from Tim and pulled harder.

"Come on, Poppy," she said.

"There are people waiting."

Poppy growled.

Then Dad got off the boat, put his
arms underneath Poppy, and carried
her onto the boat.

The boat finally left the pier and
headed out of the harbor.

"We're on the open sea, Poppy!"
Tim said.

I'm a pirate dog now! Poppy thought.

Then the boat hit a big wave and water sprayed over the side.

Poppy hid in the corner away from the waves and the slippery puddles.

"What's the matter with her?" Suzy asked.

"Maybe she doesn't like fishing," Tim said.

"The water is a little rough today," said Mom.

Poppy agreed.

"Well, that was fun, wasn't it?"
Dad said as they walked back.

Poppy wobbled along behind
them, her tail between her legs. She
didn't feel very well.

*Fishing trips are not the kind of
thing pirate dogs enjoy,* she
decided.

Four

By the time Poppy woke up the next morning, she was ready to try again. *That wasn't really my kind of boat,* she told herself. *After all, it was a smelly old fishing boat. Not a pirate ship.*

The family went down to the
harbor for the seal-spotting trip.

This boat looks newer, Poppy
thought. *Much nicer and smoother.*

As they waited in line, Poppy hoped no one would notice that her tail had stopped wagging. *I'm excited,* she told herself.

"Hey, look at that," the seal-trip man said. "We've got a pirate with us today."

"That's right," Suzy said. "She's Poppy, the Pirate Dog."

The seal-trip man smiled. "On you go, then, Poppy, the Pirate Dog," he said.

Poppy held her breath, closed her eyes . . . and leaped onto the ship!

Poppy put her paws on the rail
between Tim and Suzy.

This was more like it. The sea
was calm, and the boat rode smoothly
across the water. *Look at me,* she
thought. *I'm a pirate dog!* She was
strong. She was brave. She was—

Aaarrrggghhhhh! —

hiding under a bench.

"Tim, look at Poppy," Suzy said.
"I think she's scared."

*You'd be scared, too, if you'd seen
what I just saw,* Poppy thought. *An
enormous sea monster!*

"Look, Suzy," Tim called, pointing
at the sea monster.

"A cute little seal!" Suzy said.

Poppy decided that seal-spotting
trips were not the kind of thing pirate
dogs enjoyed, either.

"Do you think we should leave her at home today?" Mom asked the next morning.

Poppy let out a whimper and grabbed her leash.

"I think she wants to come," Tim said. "It's pedal boats — nice and slow."

Maybe pedal boats will be the perfect boats for pirate dogs, Poppy thought.

But it turned out that pedal boats were not the kind of thing pirate dogs liked.

And the next day, Poppy
discovered that speedboats weren't the
kind of boats pirate dogs liked, either.

Poppy wasn't feeling very much
like a pirate dog anymore.

That night, when Dad fed Poppy her dinner, she barely sniffed it before she walked off to bed.

They only had two days of vacation left! Would she ever find her pirate ship?

CHAPTER
Five

The next morning, Poppy was still miserable. Mom and Dad thought a day at the beach might help cheer her up.

The beach was full of people playing. But when Tim kicked a ball to Poppy, she didn't even try to chase it.

And when Dad threw a Frisbee, she just watched it float by.

"What's wrong with Poppy?" asked Suzy.

"I think I know what's the matter with her!" Tim said. "Poppy's a pirate dog, and we haven't found her the perfect pirate ship."

Poppy's tail gave a little wag.

"I think you might be right," Suzy said. "But we've only got one day left, and we've already tried all the boats in the harbor!"

"There's got to be something else," Tim said. "We have to try."

That night, everyone searched through magazines and pamphlets, trying to find the perfect pirate ship for Poppy.

Finally Mom said, "I've got it—just the thing!"

So the next morning, they all jumped in the car and headed to the last boat.

Poppy was nervous. What if the same thing happened again? What if she wasn't a pirate dog after all?

They parked beside a peaceful
river and a man came over to show
them the boat.

"There it is," he said.

"She's a beauty," Dad said.

Suzy turned to Poppy. "What do
you think?" she asked.

Poppy looked at the boat and lifted her ears. This looked like her kind of pirate ship!

"Go on board," Tim said.

Poppy stepped across the wooden plank onto the boat.

She stood on the deck and
wagged her tail at the parrot.

She poked her head through the
window and barked.

She ran to the bow.

"Look!" Suzy called, pointing at Poppy's tail. "She likes it!"

Poppy's tail was wagging so hard, it nearly knocked over a plant!

Dad started the engine, with

Poppy proudly beside him.

"We've found Poppy's perfect pirate ship!" Tim said.

Yes, Poppy thought. *It's exactly the right size, it's not too fast, and there are no big scary sea monsters.*

*This is **exactly** the right kind of ship for a pirate dog,* Poppy thought.

And when they got back home that night, Poppy curled up and fell asleep, already dreaming of her next pirate-dog adventure.